Carrots for Charlie

A Tale of Health, Fitness and Happiness

RHONDA BRAZINA and IDA R. MARGOLIS
Illustrated by VIRGINIA C. MULFORD

Barringer Publishing, Naples, Florida
www.barringerpublishing.com
Cover, graphics, layout design by Lisa Camp

ISBN: 978-0-9851184-6-4

Library of Congress Cataloging-in-Publication Data
Carrots for Charlie / Rhonda Brazina and Ida R. Margolis

Printed in U.S.A.

This is a work of fiction. All characters, organizations,
and events portrayed in this story are either products of the
authors' imagination or are used fictitiously.

A portion of the proceeds of this book
will go to KisforKids® Foundation.

Dedications

To my husband Steve,
my book loving daughters Michelle and Danielle.
Love you forever.
~Rhonda

To my husband Jeff,
my daughter Jamibeth and
my mother who valued education.
~Ida

To my children and
their children's children.
~Virginia

A happy song, a walk, and a smile was how Max started each day in his beautiful hometown of Naples, Florida. Max loved to sing and make up his own songs.

I sing a tune as I take a walk.
I smile at people and stop to talk.
It's healthy to eat an apple when I rise.
I feel so good when I exercise.

One day Max read in the newspaper that there were many dogs at the local shelter that needed homes.

The next day Max went to the shelter. Max saw a little brown and white dog with sad eyes. It was love at first sight!

Louise was in charge of adoptions at the shelter. Louise told Max,

"This dog is loveable and lots of fun.
He needs to exercise and he needs to run.
Charlie is his name, please keep it the same.
Be sure his weight stays just right,
And here's a book about his breed to read tonight."

Max said, "Charlie is a perfect name for my new dog. Louise, I will read the book that you gave me and I promise to take good care of Charlie."

Max took Charlie home. He put out a bowl of fresh water and a serving of dog food. Max gave Charlie a warm bath. Max then sang a song about rules that the little dog would need to know.

When riding in the elevator, down and up,
You will be carried like a little pup.
Following rules is always good,
So you must wear your leash in the neighborhood.

Charlie's favorite time of day was walking and running with Max and listening to him sing. Charlie loved the special song that Max would sing to him as they walked to the park.

Charlie, my buddy, my best friend you are,
I will love you and feed you, and never be far.

Max and Charlie spent time outdoors every day. Charlie's favorite places were the Naples Dog Park, outdoor concerts in Cambier Park, walking down Third Avenue to the farmers' market, and playing catch. A very special time for Charlie was eating lunch with Max at their favorite restaurant on 5th Avenue, and also going to Yappy Hour at Venetian Village.

One of Max's neighbors heard him singing. She asked Max if he would give her singing lessons. Soon Max had so many students that Charlie was left home alone most of the day. Charlie had plenty of food, water and treats. Max left the TV tuned to Animal Planet to keep Charlie entertained. Charlie missed his playtime with Max.

When Charlie was not watching TV or napping, he spent his
time eating. Charlie was so bored staying home all day.

Max was working so much that now Charlie's only outdoor time was two short walks a day. One day while walking, Max saw his friends Carlos and Amy with their children, Jake and Julie. Carlos said, "Max, your dog is moving slower than he used to."

"Charlie does not look so good. Charlie looks chubby," Jake said.

"Shhh," said Julie, "Don't hurt Charlie's feelings."

"You know both Jake and Julie are fond of your dog. They don't mean to hurt his feelings," said Amy.

"We all love Charlie. Maybe you should have the vet check him," said Carlos.

Max took Charlie to the vet. "Spaniels like Charlie must get lots of exercise and be careful to eat the right foods," said the Doctor.

"Extra weight could hurt Charlie's back and knees and is not good for his heart."

The vet added, "Vegetables are good for dogs. Charlie's new treats could be carrots and apples cut into bite size pieces."

Max knew that both he and Charlie had eaten too many treats and were not getting enough exercise.

On the way home Max saw a sign that said, *"Jiggle Butt Jym™ Fitness Center For Dogs and Their Friends."*

This was just the place for Charlie and Max. Dressed in matching clothes, Max sang to Charlie while they walked fast on the treadmill.

> *Walking, running and working out*
> *Now make us happy, we don't pout.*
> *Going to the gym is not work, it's fun*
> *And exercise is important for everyone!*

Soon everyone in the Jiggle Butt Jym was singing along with Max.

After a healthy and yummy dinner, Max put small pieces of apples and carrots in Charlie's bowl instead of sweet treats. He did this day after day.

A few weeks later Max was sitting on the sofa and noticed the sofa was feeling lumpy. He lifted up the sofa cushions. Guess what he saw? Piles and piles of carrots! Charlie had eaten the apples, but had hidden all of the carrots under the sofa cushions.

Max did not know what to do. Then he remembered the dog book Louise had given him. The answer was in the book.

...Dogs might like vegetables if mixed with a little plain yogurt...

Max tried this and it worked. After Charlie ate the carrots and yogurt, a cheerful Max wrote a new song.

> *Carrots and apples are our new treat.*
> *The others were not healthy and much too sweet.*
> *Eating fresh foods will make us feel great.*
> *And exercising together will help with our weight.*

Charlie was happy to be walking and running and doing fun things with Max again. As they walked to an outdoor concert everyone stopped to see the little dog with the happy eyes. Even the Mayor smiled and waved at Charlie as he walked by.

Max then saw Amy with her children, Jake and Julie. They were all proud of the way Max and Charlie worked hard to be healthy.

After the concert, Jake and Julie could hardly keep up with Max and Charlie as they all went to the farmers' market. They bought fruits and vegetables and lots of Charlie's new favorite, carrots.

It was time to take Charlie back to the vet. The doctor said, "Hooray! Charlie now weighs just the right amount and has a strong heart. You fed him healthy food and took him on long fun walks. Good job."

Max went right to his friends' house to tell them what the vet said. Carlos, Amy and their children were happy to hear that Charlie was strong and healthy. Max then taught them a new song so that they could all sing together as they played with Charlie.

Carrots, apples and yogurt are treats for us
We don't eat sweets and it's no fuss.
Eating healthy foods make us feel great.
Exercising together has helped us with our weight.

It was almost time for sunset, so Max put Charlie in the car and off they went to the Dog Beach in the nearby town of Bonita Springs. Max brought fresh crunchy orange carrots for Charlie and himself. These two best friends were now healthier and happier than they had ever been. And Charlie loved the new words to his special song.

Charlie my buddy, my real best friend you are,
I'll feed you what's healthy, I'll never be far.

Children in Naples smile, wave and shout
When they see Max with Charlie strutting about.

A few crunchy carrots and a walk in the park
Have helped Charlie and Max stay healthy,
Just hear Charlie bark!

Boys and girls join them as they walk by the Zoo,
They want to stay healthy, so they walk with them too.

When Max and Charlie walk near the Pier,
They are happy when their friends say
"We're glad that you're here!"

Questions for Discussion

1. Why was Charlie a happy dog when he first came to live with Max?

2. What changes took place in Charlie's life when Max began teaching many students?

3. What happened when Max met his friends Carlos, Amy and their children Jake and Julie?

4. What important things did the vet tell Max?

5. What changes did Max make to help Charlie get healthy and fit?

6. What was the most important thing you learned about taking care of a pet?

7. What did you learn about staying healthy from the story of Charlie and Max?

Some Facts that Charlie wants you to know about his breed
Cavalier King Charles Spaniels

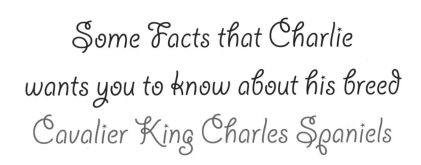

~ This breed is known to be friendly and happy when well cared for.

~ They like to be with people and are easy to train.

~ They should be given attention and brushed daily.

~ It is very important for these dogs to have a lot of exercise. The exercise can be long daily walks or romping in a large, safe yard.

~ Do NOT over feed these dogs. They gain weight easily which is not good for their health.

Dear Parents, Guardians and Teachers,

Parents and guardians play the key role in their child's nutrition and health needs. However schools, child care providers and healthcare professionals can also be important in helping to teach about health, nutrition, exercise and obesity. Obesity is now the number one health problem in the United States according to the Center for Disease Control and Prevention. One-third of all children between the ages of 2 and 19 are overweight or obese. Serious health problems can result from obesity. These problems include high blood pressure, high cholesterol, heart disease and type 2 diabetes. Also, obesity can adversely affect a child's energy level, sleep and mood.

It is widely known that it is essential to teach children about healthful eating, nutrition and the importance of physical activity. There are a great variety of resources available on these topics. Excellent books are available in book stores and libraries. The Internet has hundreds of sites that deal with nutrition, health, exercise and childhood obesity. As with all Internet information, be certain that the source is a reputable one, so you can be sure that the information provided is based on scientific research. Teachers, librarians and nutrition centers can be of assistance with websites. A brief list of resources is provided at the end of this book.

Although many resources are available about obesity and weight control it is often difficult to have a discussion with children about their weight. One purpose of this book is to facilitate a discussion about health and nutrition for children and pets.

According to the Association for Pet Obesity Prevention (APOP) over 50% of all dogs and cats in the U.S. are overweight or obese. There are many health risks to pets that are associated with excess weight just as there are health risks associated with excess weight in children and adults. We hope that reading about Charlie and Max can help children understand the importance of following a healthful diet and keeping physically active.

Websites

www.cdc.gov/obesity
Center for Disease Control and Prevention, includes definitions, resources, data and recommendations.

www.ChooseMyPlate.gov
Provides practical information and tips to help Americans build healthier diets.

www.cspinet.org
Center for Science in the Public Interest, provides information about food and health.

www.diabetes.org
American Diabetes Association, includes information about diabetes, food, fitness and research.

www.healthiergeneration.org
Alliance for a Healthier Generation, provides outstanding information aimed toward helping today's children become healthier.

www.letsmove.gov
"America's Move to Raise a Healthier Generation of Kids," includes excellent information on food, nutrition, and physical activity.

Websites

www.nutrition.gov

Provides easy, online access to government information on food and human nutrition for consumers.

www.petobesityprevention.com

Association for Pet Obesity Prevention is committed to making lives of dogs, cats and all other animals and people healthier and more vital.

www.Bumblesonline.com

Original children's music group promoting health and encouraging good habits.

The above web sites have much up to date, great information.

A fun activity could be to pick one favorite tip from each site. For example, Max's favorite tip from www.nutrition.gov is to read food labels carefully. "Food labels help consumers make healthier choices."

Charlie's favorite tip from www.petobesityprevention.com is that people should not feed pets fried food, pizza or chicken wings when having a party. Instead they should feed their pet a crunchy vegetable... and you know what vegetable is Charlie's favorite.

Recipes

These healthful recipes for children
are courtesy of the 6th Grade Students
in Mrs. Brock's Family and Consumer Science Classes
at Pine Ridge Middle School, Naples, Florida

Mr. Max's Macaroni Salad

1 16 ounce package whole grain or high protein pasta
1 large carrot, cut into strips
1 green pepper, chopped
½ cup frozen peas, thawed
10 cherry tomatoes
½ cup black olives, sliced
¾ cup light Italian dressing

1. Cook pasta according to package directions. Drain and rinse in cold water.

2. In a large bowl combine all vegetables with the pasta.

3. Add dressing then stir.

4. Refrigerate for two hours. Stir again.

5. Eat and enjoy!

Peanut Butter Banana Wraps

1 package of whole wheat tortilla wraps (10-12 inch)
Peanut Butter
Fruit spread (a jam with no added sugar)
1 banana per wrap (peeled)

1. Spread peanut butter edge to edge on each wrap. Next spread the sugar-free jam on the peanut butter. (This is optional)

2. Beginning at one side of the wrap, roll the wrap around the banana. This could be eaten easily with one hand as a simple snack or lunch "sandwich."

3. For fun or serving on a platter slice the "roll" into 1 to 1½" individual pieces. These look very nice for a party and are fun bite size snacks.

Fruit Kabobs

Strawberries, Pineapples, Watermelon, Grapes, Melon
Package of 6-8" skewers

1. Wash all fruit.

2. Cut tops of strawberries.

3. Cut pineapple and melons into 3/4–1" cubes.

4. Put fruit on skewers alternating different colored fruit.

Carlos' Tortilla Pizzas

1 package of whole wheat tortilla wraps
1 jar of pizza sauce without "added sugar"
Package of low fat shredded cheese of your choice
(or mix together a cheddar and mozzarella combination)
An assortment of your favorite veggies for the topping cut
into small bite size pieces
Mushrooms, peppers, tomatoes, zucchini work well.

1. Place each tortilla on a cookie sheet or pizza baking tray sprayed lightly with some vegetable spray.

2. Put several spoonfuls of the pizza sauce on the tortilla and spread to about ½" from the edges. Top with a handful of cheese and then add another handful of the chopped vegetables spread across the entire wrap.

3. Bake at 350 degrees until the cheese melts and it has a slight brown color on the top.

Carefully move the hot tortilla to a cutting board using a large spatula

Can be served as an individual pizza or cut into slices.

Use a pizza cutting wheel for safe cutting. Ask an adult to help with cutting if you have never done it before.

Acknowledgements

A special thank you to all of our incredible friends and relatives who gave generously of their time and talent in the reading and re-reading of this book.

Thank you to all those in the community who have embraced our mission to promote nutrition and exercise for children and encouraged us. A special thank you to our publisher, Jeff and to Naples Mayor John Sorey.